This book belongs to:

....

....

....

Retold by Gaby Goldsack
Illustrated by Emma Lake
Designed by Jester Designs

Language consultant: Betty Root

ISBN 1-84461-311-9

Marks and Spencer p.l.c.
PO Box 3339
Chester, CH99 9QS
www.marksandspencer.com

Sleeping Beauty

Helping your Child to Read

Learning to read is an exciting challenge for most
children. From a very early age, sharing story books with
children, talking about the pictures and guessing what
might happen next are all very important parts of the
reading experience.

Sharing reading

Set aside a regular quiet time to share reading with
younger children, or to be on hand to encourage older
children as they develop into independent readers.

First Readers are intended to encourage and support the
early stages of learning to read. They present
well-loved tales that children will happily listen to again
and again. Familiarity helps children to identify some of
the words and phrases.

When you feel your child is ready to move on a little, encourage him or her to join in so that you read the story aloud together. Always pause to talk about the pictures. The easy-to-read speech bubbles in **First Readers** provide an excellent 'joining-in' activity. The bright, clear illustrations and matching text will help children to understand the story.

Building confidence

In time, children will want to read *to* you. When this happens, be patient and give continual praise. They may not read all the words correctly, but children's substitutions are often very good guesses.

The repetition in each book is particularly helpful for building confidence. If your child cannot read a particular word, go back to the beginning of the sentence and read it together so the meaning is not lost. Most importantly, do not continue if your child is tired or simply in need of a change.

Reading alone

The next step is to ask your child to read alone. Try to be on hand to give help and support. Remember to give lots of encouragement and praise.

Together with other simple stories, **First Readers** will ensure that children will find reading an enjoyable and rewarding experience.

Long ago a king and queen
wanted a baby.

One day their dream came true.

We must
have a party.

They had a baby girl. She was lovely.
The king and queen were happy.
"Everyone in the land must see the new
princess," said the queen.
"We must have a party," said the king.

Everyone in the land came to the party.

Four good fairies came to see
the new princess.

They waved their wands.

They cast their spells.

"She will be beautiful,"
said the first.

"She will be wise," said the second.

"She will be kind,"
said the third.

Just then there was a puff of smoke.

It was the wicked fairy.

"How dare you forget to invite me!" cried the wicked fairy.
The king and queen had forgotten to invite her.

We forgot!

The wicked fairy waved her wand. She cast a wicked spell.

"The princess will prick her finger on a spinning wheel and die!" she cried.

14

There was a puff of smoke.

The wicked fairy disappeared.

The king and queen were sad.

The fourth fairy waved her wand.

"I cannot break the wicked spell,"
she said. "But I can change it.
When the princess pricks her finger
she will not die.
She will sleep for one hundred years.
A kiss from a prince will wake her."

17

The king got rid of all the spinning
wheels in the land.

Many years passed. The princess grew
up to be beautiful, wise and kind.

One day, the princess wanted to
explore the castle.

At the top of a tower she found
a dusty room.

In the room was a dusty spinning wheel.

The princess dusted the spinning wheel with her finger.

"Ouch!" She pricked her finger on the spinning wheel.

The princess fell into a deep sleep.

Everyone in the castle fell asleep.

One hundred years passed. Thorns grew around the castle.

One day, a prince came riding by.
He wanted to explore the castle.
He cut his way through the thorns.

The prince found the dusty room
at the top of the tower.
He found the princess asleep.

The princess was beautiful.
The prince kissed her.

The princess woke up at once.
She looked at the prince.
He had broken the spell.

Everyone in the castle woke up.
Soon after, the prince and princess
were married.
Everyone in the land came
to the wedding.

27

Read and Say

How many of these words can you say?
The pictures will help you. Look back in
your book and see if you can find the
words in the story.

fairy

king

queen

baby

princess

prince

wand

castle

spinning wheel

finger

Titles in this series,
subject to availability:

Beauty and the Beast
Chicken-Licken
Cinderella
The Elves and the Shoemaker
The Emperor's New Clothes
The Enormous Turnip
The Gingerbread Man
Goldilocks and the Three Bears
Hansel and Gretel
Jack and the Beanstalk
Joseph's Coat of Many Colours
Little Red Riding Hood
Noah's Ark and other Bible Stories
Rapunzel
Rumpelstiltskin
Sleeping Beauty
Snow White and the Seven Dwarfs
The Three Billy Goats Gruff
The Three Little Pigs
The Ugly Duckling